TEN RULES

OF BEING A

SUPERHERO

Deb Pilutti

Christy Ottaviano Books

Henry Holt and Company ☆ New York

For Kathy, Tim, Mark, and Dan,
who have all worn a cape at
one time or another

Henry Holt and Company, LLC
Publishers since 1866
175 Fifth Avenue
New York, New York 10010
mackids.com

Henry Holt® is a registered trademark of Henry Holt and Company, LLC.
Copyright © 2014 by Deb Pilutti
All rights reserved.

Library of Congress Cataloging-in-Publication Data is available.

ISBN 978-0-8050-9759-7

Henry Holt books may be purchased for business or promotional use.
For information on bulk purchases, please contact Macmillan Corporate
and Premium Sales Department at (800) 221-7945 x5442 or by e-mail
at specialmarkets@macmillan.com.

First Edition—2014
The illustrations for this book were done in gouache.
Printed in China by Macmillan Production (Asia) Ltd.,
Kowloon Bay, Hong Kong (Vendor Code: 10)

10 9 8 7 6 5 4 3

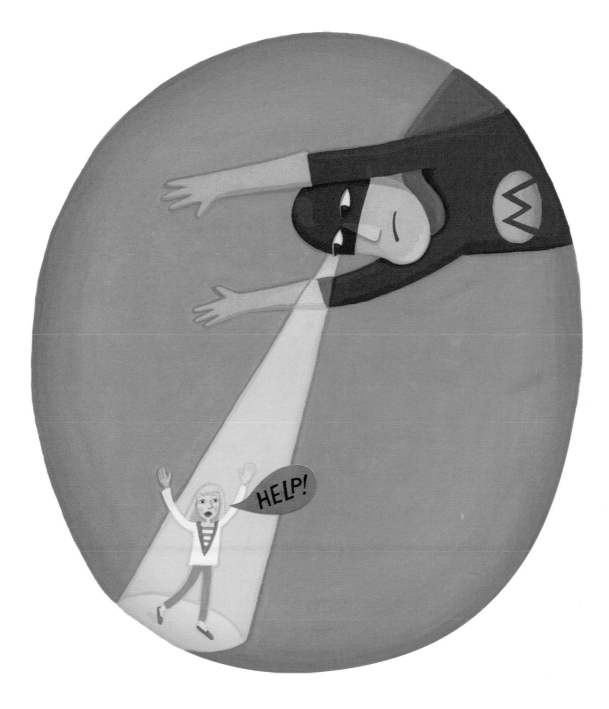

Rule NUMBER 1

A superhero must ALWAYS respond to a call for help . . .

even if the odds are against him.

Rule Number 2

Saving the day is messy.

But everyone understands.

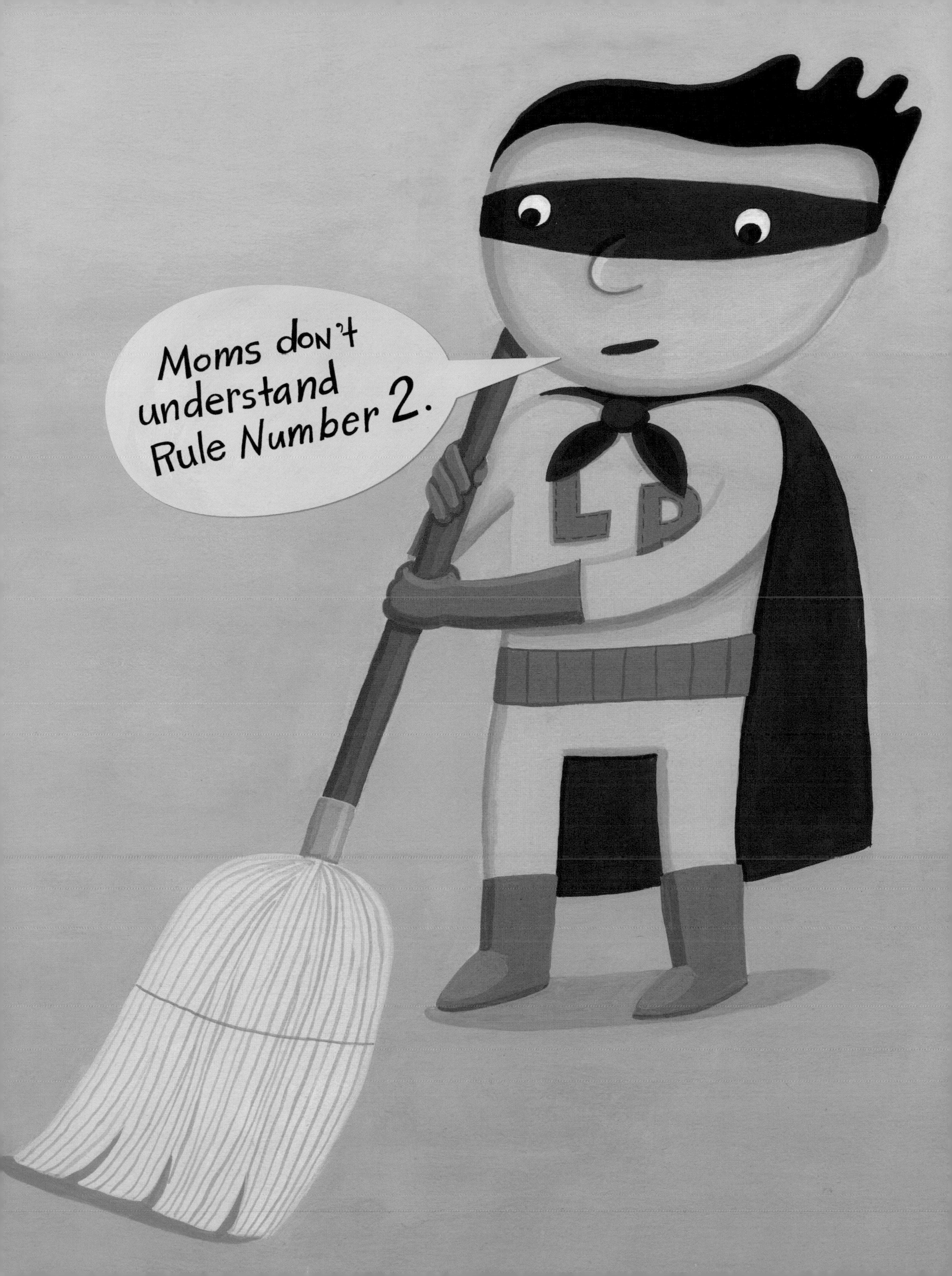
Moms don't understand Rule Number 2.

Rule NUMBER 3

Every superhero has at least one superpower.
That's what makes him

SUPER!

Captain
Magma
has three.

He is really
strong,

has lava vision,

and a friendly personality.

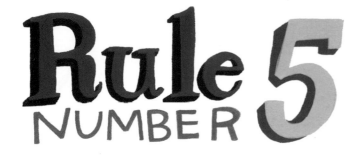

Rule NUMBER 5

Sometimes superheroes make a lot of noise.

Not everyone appreciates this rule.

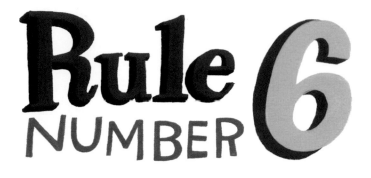

Rule NUMBER 6

A superhero needs
a tasty snack to be in

TOP
FORM.

Rule NUMBER 7

Superheroes must rest so that they can recharge . . .

and be ready when the time comes to save the day.

Help.

HELP!

Like now.

HeLLo-o!

EXCUSE ME!!

YOO- HOO!

Could you give me a hand?

Rule
NUMBER 8

A superhero is
always brave.

Well, ALMOST always.

Rule NUMBER 9

The goal of a superhero is to save innocent victims.

Not this Worm, Mr. Bird!

With no thought for his own safety.

Rule NUMBER 10

Every superhero
needs a sidekick.

Because saving the day is
more fun with a friend.